TO BEN & JET

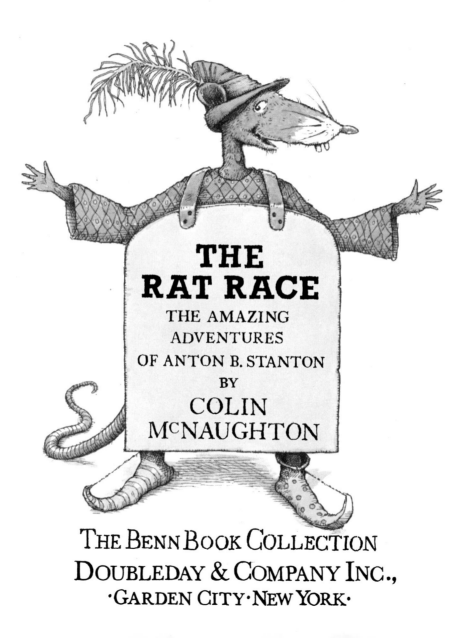

THE RAT RACE

THE AMAZING ADVENTURES
OF ANTON B. STANTON

BY

COLIN McNAUGHTON

THE BENN BOOK COLLECTION

DOUBLEDAY & COMPANY INC.,

·GARDEN CITY·NEW YORK·

Benn Book
COLLECTION

The Benn Book Collection
Published by Doubleday & Company Inc.,
Garden City, New York

Text and illustrations
Copyright © 1978 Colin McNaughton
All rights reserved
First edition in the United States
of America
Printed in England

Library of Congress
Catalog Card Number 77-82648

**Library of Congress Cataloging
in Publication Data**
  McNaughton, Colin
The Rat Race

  "The Benn Book Collection"
  Summary: A very small boy imprisoned
in the city of rats enters the rat race
in hopes of becoming king for one day.
  [1. Rats – Fiction]
I. Title.
PZY.M23256Rat [E] 77–82648

ISBN 0–385–13619–6 (Trade)
       0–385–13620–X (Prebound)

Ladies and gentlemen, our hero.

A small boy by the name of Anton B. Stanton.
Now when I say small...

...I mean small.

This is Anton with his family. They all lived together in a huge castle.

Because of his size Anton couldn't join in with his
brothers' games. He just got in the way.

One day, Anton was
feeling especially
bored. Suddenly, he saw
an odd looking rat. It
disappeared into a hole in the wall

and without thinking, he followed it.

The tunnel went on and on, until finally, Anton saw a light at the end. "At last," thought Anton. But he was not prepared for the sight which met his eyes. A city of rats!

"What's this, then?" said a voice. And two rats grabbed him by the arms. "Looks like we've caught ourselves a spy, Olaf," said one. "Indeed it does, Nolaf. We'd better take him to the king. We'll get a medal for this."

Olaf and Nolaf marched a bewildered Anton
through the city.

Finally, they arrived at the palace.
Anton was taken into the Royal Presence.

"On your knees!" whispered Olaf to Anton.
"We've caught a spy, Your Majesty.
He was trying to sneak into the city."
"But I'm not a spy," protested Anton.

"Silence!" shouted the king, who was a great practical joker. "I sentence you to 496 years in prison; one year for spying and 495 years for being so ugly." The courtiers thought this so funny they all fell about laughing.

Anton was taken away and put into a dark
and dingy cell.

In the next room, he could hear Olaf and Nolaf,
who had been given the job of guarding him,
talking very excitedly about a race.

"Excuse me, but, what *is* all this about a race?"
asked Anton. They were showing him a poster, when the
king walked in with medals for Olaf and Nolaf. Suddenly,
Anton had an idea. "Your Majesty," said Anton,
"can anyone run in the race?"

"Of course," answered the king. "Why do you ask?"
"Well," explained Anton. "If I win, I'll be king for a day
and the first thing I'll do is to set myself free." The king
chuckled. "Never let it be said that King Rattus III
was not a sportsman. You may race," he said.

As soon as the king left, Anton started training.

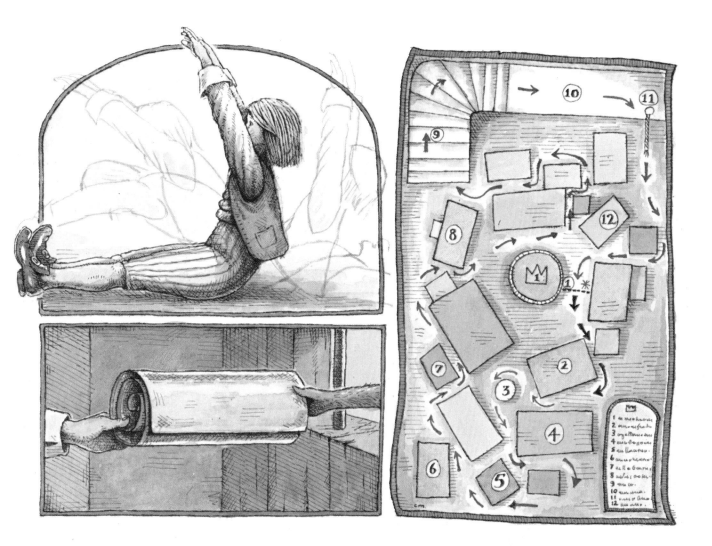

Olaf gave him a map of the course.

On the day of the race, the whole town turned out to watch.
It was obvious to Anton who was his greatest rival:
Number 9, a big burly rat named Gruffaw.

The king raised his flag and shouted, "On your marks, get set, GO!" They were off.

Straightaway, Anton went out in front; but not for long. Someone had tripped him up.

Meanwhile, Gruffaw stormed into the lead.

Anton picked himself up, feeling very wobbly indeed,

and started to run. But soon his strength returned.

One by one he passed the other competitors,

until he reached the staircase, with no one ahead but Gruffaw.

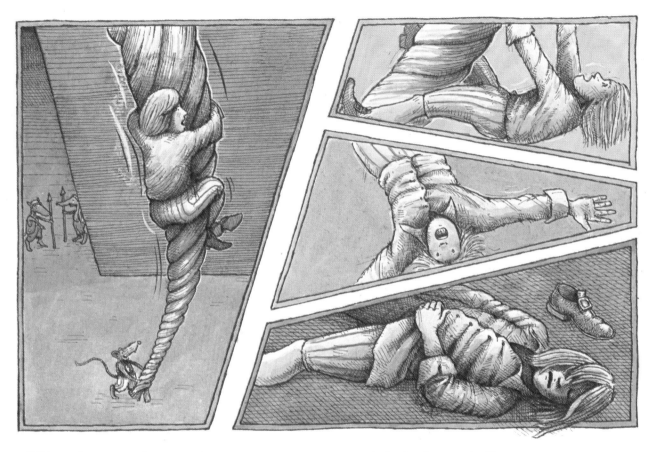

The last obstacle was a rope which hung from
the landing at the top of the stairs. Anton was
half way down when Gruffaw started shaking the rope.
Anton simply could not hold on.

Laughing, Gruffaw ran off towards the finishing line.
Fortunately, Olaf and Nolaf had seen the whole thing
and they helped Anton to his feet.

So Gruffaw's glory did not last long.
Olaf and Nolaf told the king what had happened
and Gruffaw was disgraced. He was given third prize,
which did not please him one little bit.

Anton was declared the winner and spent a lovely day
as king of the rats. When the time came for him to leave,
he was more than a little sad; but as Nolaf tearfully said,
"All good things must come to an end."

Anton's family were overjoyed to see him again.
"We looked for you all over the castle," they cried.
"Where <u>have</u> you been?"
"To see the king," he told them.
"Oh Anton," they laughed. "Whatever will you think of nex